Is that you, George?

Kate Oliver

Blackie
London

Bedrick/Blackie
New York

To Jenny and David

British Library Cataloguing in Publication Data

Oliver, Kate
    Is that you, George?
    I. Title
    823′.914

ISBN 0–216–92784–6

First American edition published in 1990 by
Peter Bedrick Books
2112 Broadway, Rm. 318
New York, NY 10023

Library of Congress Cataloging-in-Publication Data

Oliver, Kate.
    Is that you, George?/Kate Oliver.—1st American ed.
        p.   cm.
        Summary: Bored with being sick in bed, George becomes a polar bear
    for a day, much to his parents' dismay.
        ISBN 0-87226-422-X
        [1. Polar bear—Fiction. 2. Bears—Fiction. 3. Sick—Fiction.]
    I. Title.
    PZ7.0474Is   1990
    [E]—dc20   89-18002
                                                                      CIP
                                                                       AC

Blackie and Son Ltd
7 Leicester Place
London WC2H 7BP

Printed in Hong Kong

George is bored.
He has got a cold and is spending the day in bed.

In the evening Dad reads him a bedtime story about the North Pole.

George falls asleep and dreams.

Next morning when Mum brings in George's breakfast she finds . . .

. . . a polar bear!

Mum drops the breakfast tray with a CRASH! and runs to fetch Dad.

   The polar bear wakes up.

In the doorway he sees Mum, Dad, Lucy, baby James
and Sally the dog. They all stare at the polar bear,
and the polar bear stares back.

'Is that you, George?' asks Dad nervously.

The polar bear grunts and nods.

'Well, you'd better get up and come downstairs for some breakfast, then,' says Mum.

George gets out of bed. He tries to walk on two legs but is very wobbly, so he walks on all fours instead.

When he looks in the mirror on the landing, George is *very* surprised to see a polar bear staring back at him.

Oh, well, being a polar bear might be fun, thinks George, and he makes his way downstairs.

In the sitting-room he switches on the television
to watch his favourite Saturday morning cartoons.

'Breakfast's ready,' says Lucy, and leads
him into the kitchen.

Mum pours him out some cornflakes and Dad
fetches the milk from the fridge. But George
doesn't want his cornflakes this morning.

He walks over to the freezer instead.

Mum opens the freezer door and George pulls
out a packet of fish fingers. He tears
it open, and eats the lot.
    'But you don't like fish fingers, George!'
exclaims Mum.

After breakfast Mum tells George to stay in the kitchen
while everyone goes upstairs to get dressed. But
George hears the postman coming and creeps out of
the back door to say hello.

The postman can't believe
his eyes, and runs
down the garden to
the gate, scattering
letters behind him.

Mum and Dad are very cross.

'You'd better stay inside from now on,' says Dad.

When Mum and Lucy go shopping, George wants to go, too.

'Bears aren't allowed in supermarkets,' says Dad firmly. 'You can look after baby James instead.'

When Mum and Lucy get back from the shops,
Dad cooks lunch for everyone.

George finds it rather
difficult to hold his
knife and fork, so
he eats his food
the way that Sally
eats hers. Soon
he's as messy as
baby James.

Mum and Dad are
not pleased.

After lunch Lucy goes into the garden
to play with her friends. George wants
to go, too.

'You're much too big to play in the
garden, George,' says Mum.

So George plays with his toys all afternoon instead.

After tea Dad decides it
might be a good idea for
George to have a bath —
a VERY cold bath!

Before he goes to bed, George watches
television with Lucy and Sally.

When he is tucked up in bed, George thinks about
the day. Perhaps being a polar bear isn't much
fun after all. He can't play with his friends,
he can't go to the supermarket, and he can't even go outside.

Mum comes in and reads George a story. Then she kisses him goodnight and wishes him sweet dreams.

Soon George is fast asleep.

And next morning when Mum peeps in through the door – there, in bed, is . . . GEORGE!